GREENHAM COMM

MOLESWORTH,

ALCONBURY,

MILDENHALL,

LAKENHEATH,

BENTWATERS,

BRIZE NORTON,

UPPER HEYFORD,

HOLY LOCH,

MENWITH HILL,

ETC,

ETC.

A SPECIAL RELATIONSHIP
DAVID GENTLEMAN

faber and faber

LONDON · BOSTON

Other work by David Gentleman

David Gentleman's Britain
David Gentleman's London
Murals at Charing Cross underground station
British postage stamps
Cloister panels at Westminster Abbey
Posters and lithographs 1969-1986
Exhibitions of watercolours 1970-1985

First published in 1987
by Faber and Faber Limited
3 Queen Square London WC1N 3AU
Printed in Great Britain
by Jolly and Barber Limited
Rugby, Warwickshire

© 1987 David Gentleman

British Library Cataloguing in Publication data

Gentleman, David
A special relationship
1. Great Britain—Foreign relations—United States
2. United States—Foreign relations—Great Britain
3. Great Britain—Foreign relations—1945-
4. United States—Foreign relations—1945-
I. Title
327.41073   E183.8.G7

ISBN 0-571-14992-8

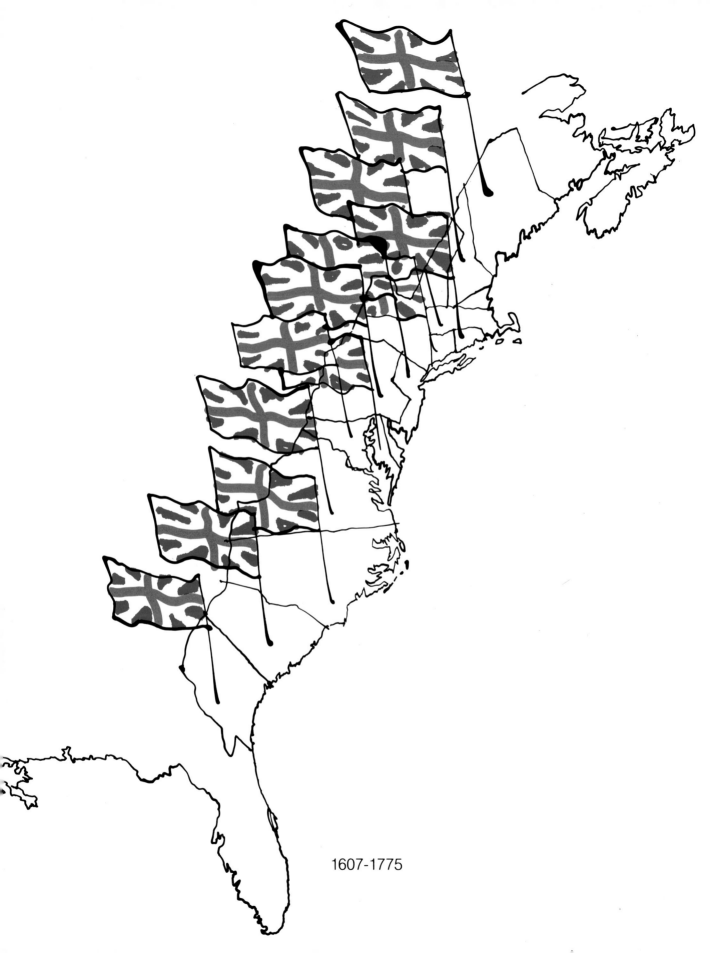

1607-1775

1776

BOSTON 1773

1800-1900

1776-1914

1914-1918

1918-1945

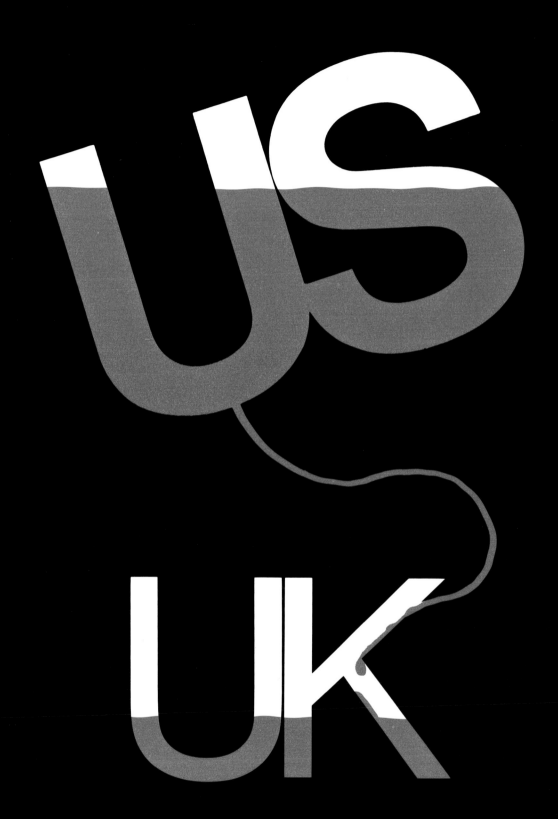

1945-1950

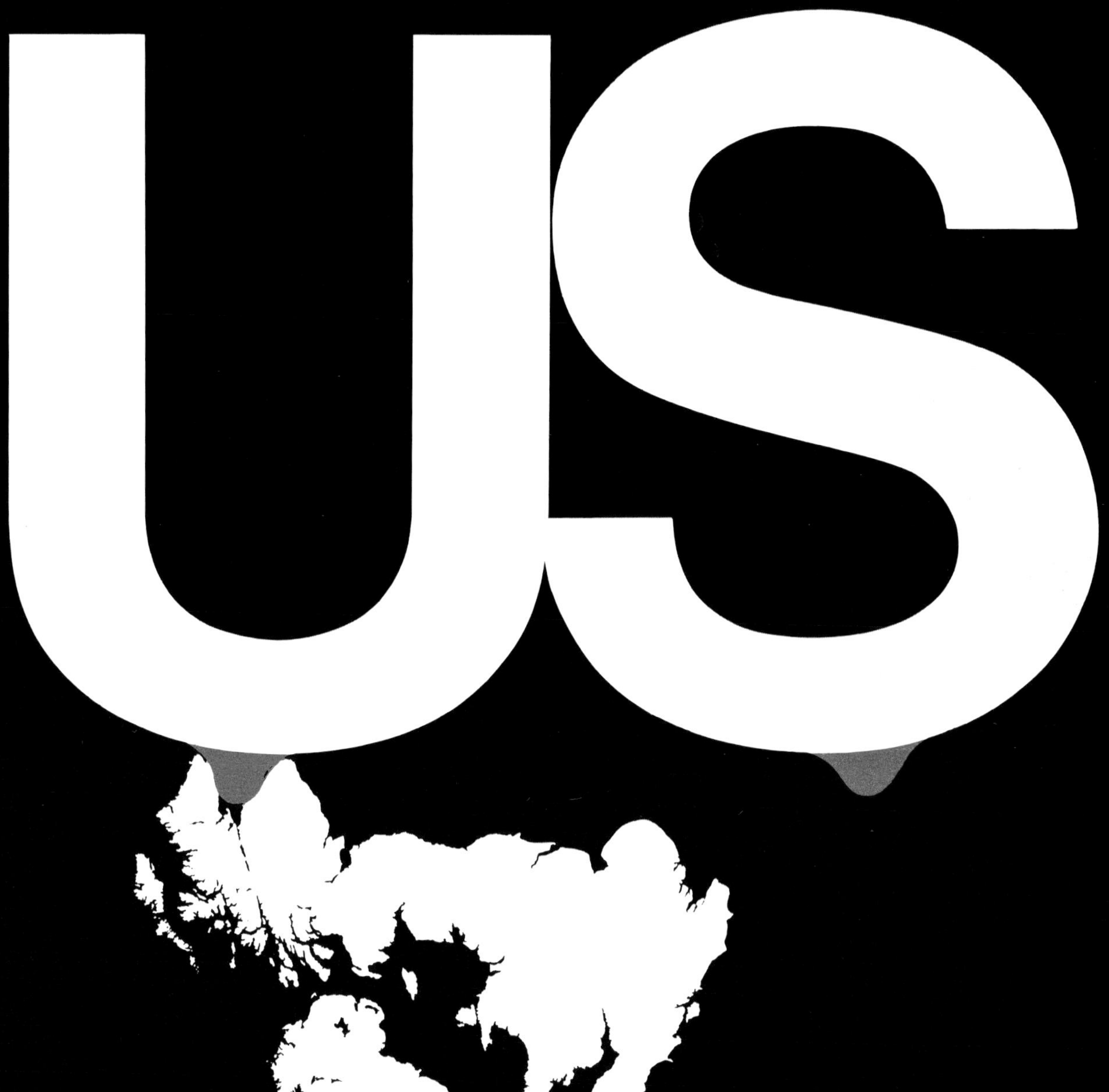
US

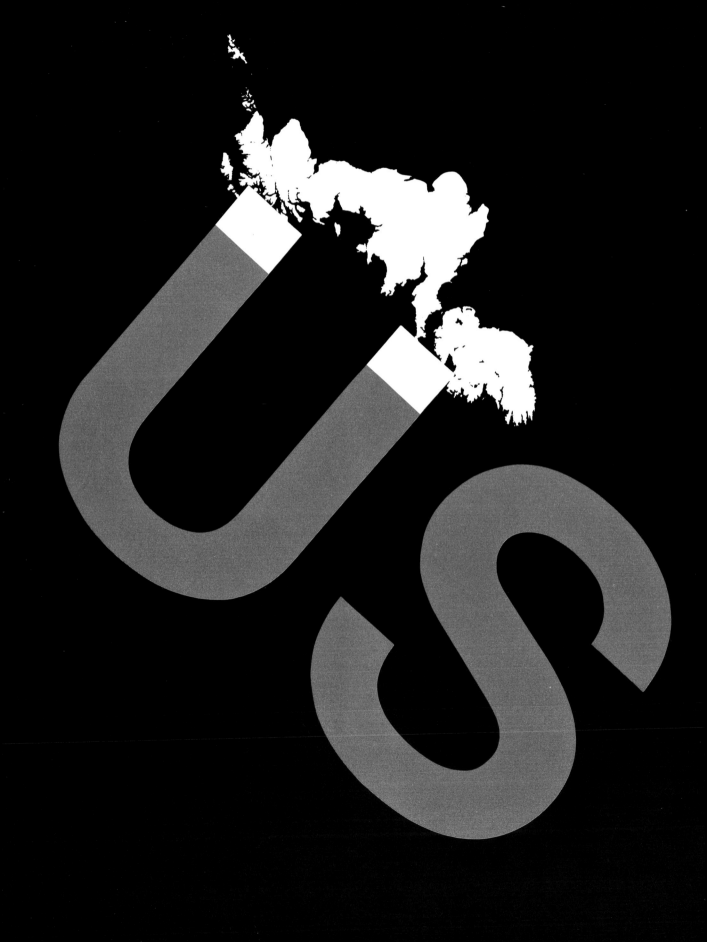

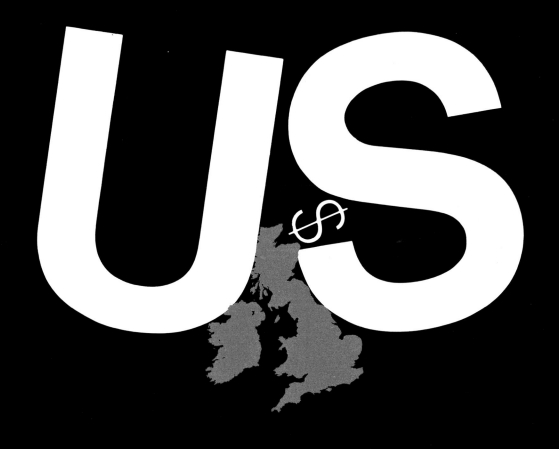

1945-1950

1950-1960

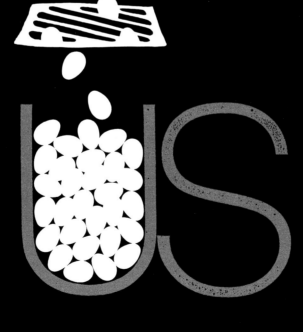

UK
US

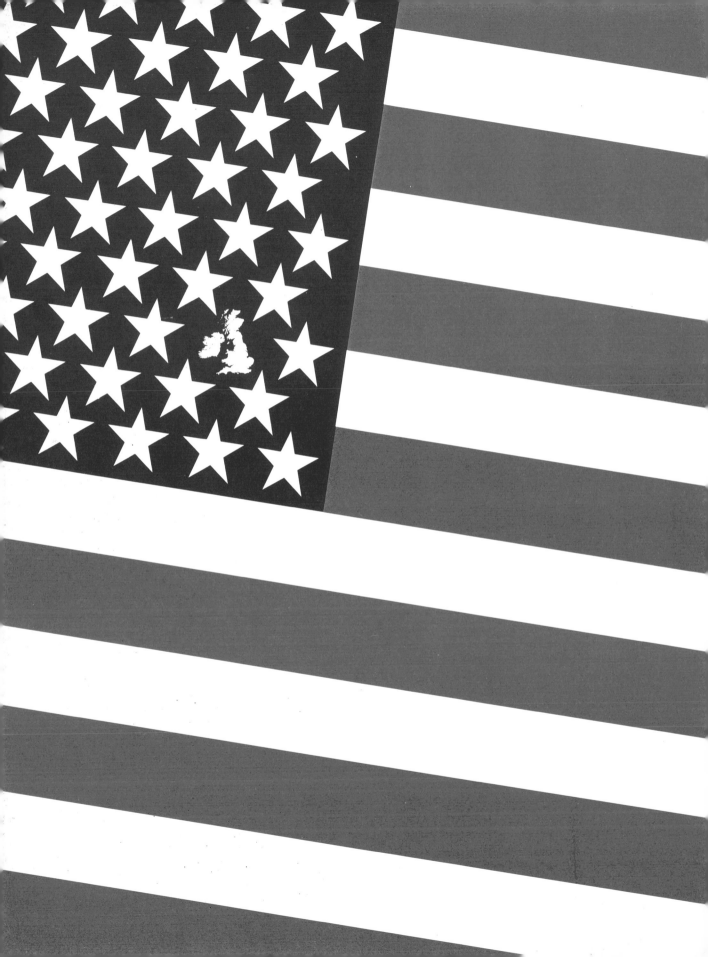

1979-1987

1982

GREENHAM COMMON 1982

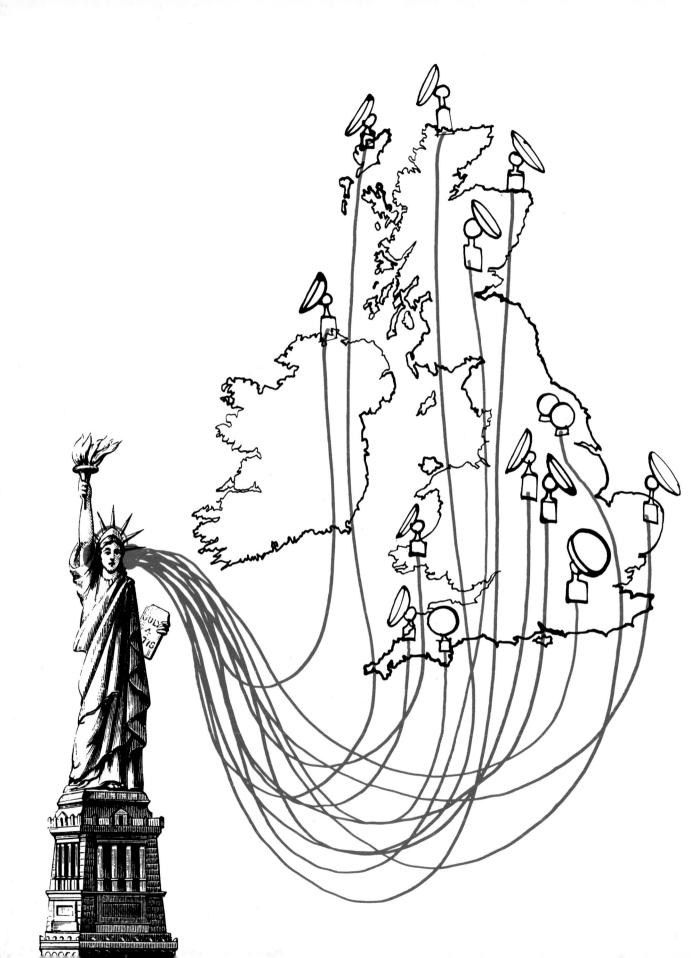

GREENHAM COMMON, MOLESWORTH

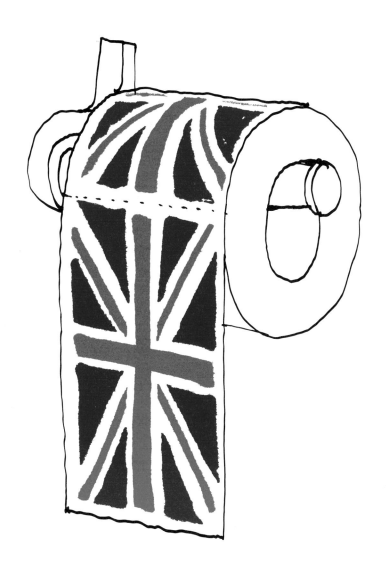

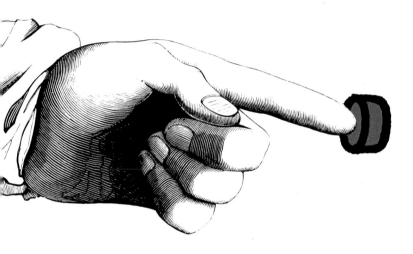

1987? 1988? 1999?

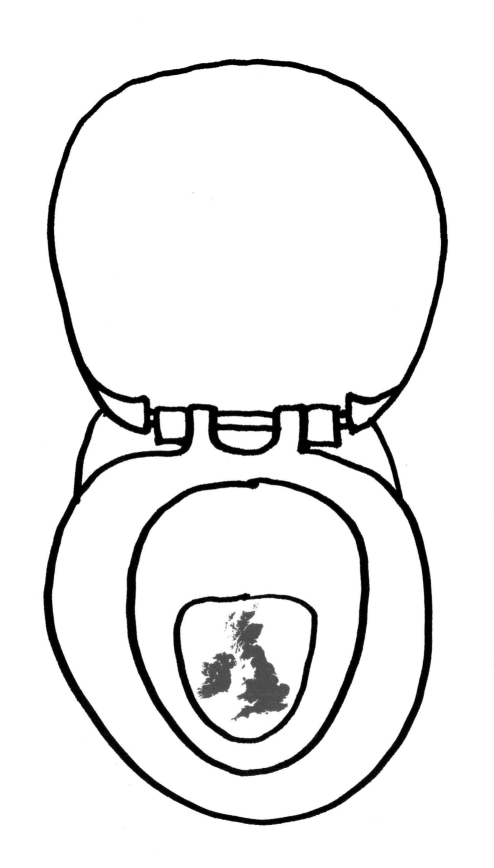

23:56

23:57

23:58

23:59

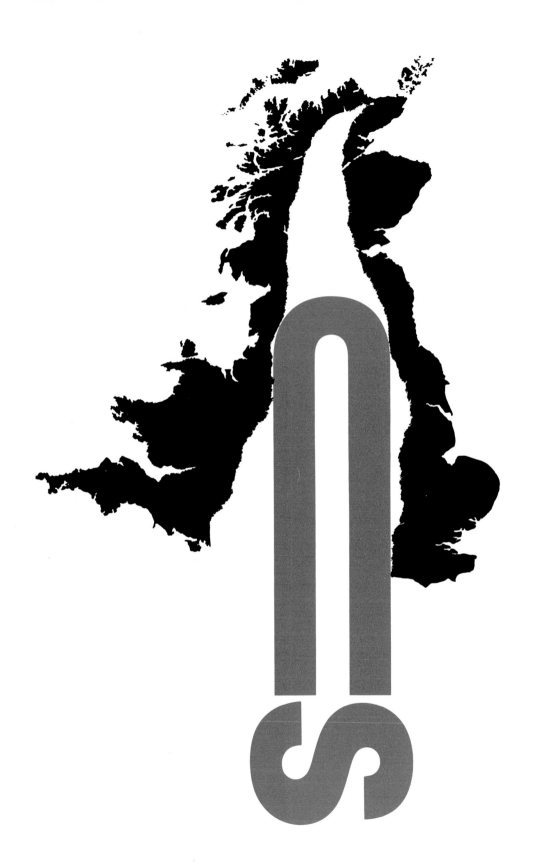

US
UK

US
UK

UK

US

V

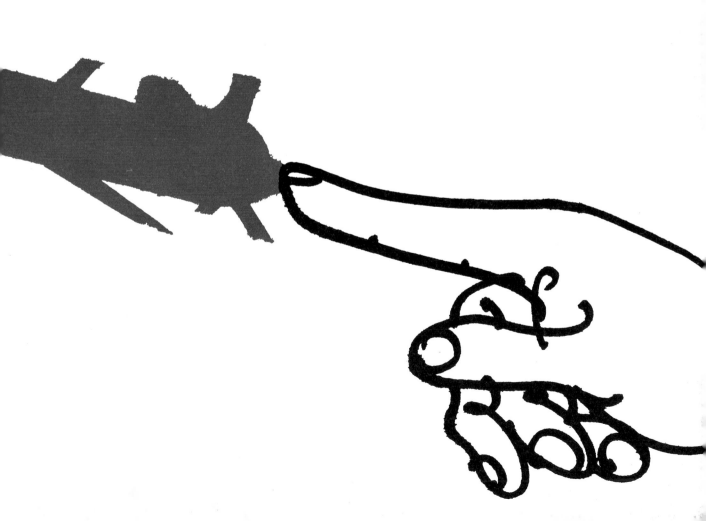

GREENHAM COMMON,

MOLESWORTH,

ALCONBURY,

MILDENHALL,

LAKENHEATH,

BENTWATERS,

BRIZE NORTON,

UPPER HEYFORD,

HOLY LOCH,

MENWITH HILL,

ETC,

ETC.